MAGIC BONE

BE CAREFUL WHAT YOU SNIFF FOR

GROSSET & DUNLAP
Published by the Penguin Group
Penguin Group (USA) Inc., 375 Hudson Street,
New York, New York 10014, USA
Penguin Group (Canada), 90 Eglinton Avenue East, Suite 700,
Toronto, Ontario M4P 2Y3, Canada
(a division of Pearson Penguin Canada Inc.)
Penguin Books Ltd, 80 Strand, London WC2R 0RL, England
Penguin Ireland, 25 St Stephen's Green, Dublin 2, Ireland
(a division of Penguin Books Ltd)
Penguin Group (Australia), 707 Collins Street,
Melbourne, Victoria 3008, Australia
(a division of Pearson Australia Group Pty Ltd)
Penguin Books India Pvt Ltd, 11 Community Centre,
Panchsheel Park, New Delhi—110 017, India
Penguin Group (NZ), 67 Apollo Drive, Rosedale, Auckland 0632, New Zealand
(a division of Pearson New Zealand Ltd)
Penguin Books (South Africa), Rosebank Office Park, 181 Jan Smuts Avenue,
Parktown North 2193, South Africa
Penguin China, B7 Jiaming Center, 27 East Third Ring Road North,
Chaoyang District, Beijing 100020, China

Penguin Books Ltd., Registered Offices:
80 Strand, London WC2R 0RL, England

Text copyright © 2013 by Nancy Krulik. Illustrations copyright © 2013
by Sebastien Braun. Published by Grosset & Dunlap, a division of
Penguin Young Readers Group, 345 Hudson Street, New York, New York 10014.
GROSSET & DUNLAP is a trademark of Penguin Group (USA) Inc.
Printed in the U.S.A.

Library of Congress Control Number: 2012027555

ISBN 978-0-448-46399-5   10 9 8 7 6 5

MAGIC
BONE

BE CAREFUL WHAT YOU SNIFF FOR

by Nancy Krulik
illustrated by Sebastien Braun

Grosset & Dunlap
An Imprint of Penguin Group (USA) Inc.

For Josie, for obvious reasons—NK

To the Dovers
and their new sweet puppy—SB

CHAPTER 1

Wiggle, waggle, wheee!

I take a flying leap and land right on the big couch in the living room. I know I'm not supposed to go on the furniture. But I can't help it—this couch is so soft and comfy.

Jiggle, jiggle, jiggle. I roll onto my back and wave my paws in the air.

Wriggle, wriggle, wriggle. I flip over and squirm on the soft cushions.

"Hello, yard!" I bark as I stand up on my back paws to look out the window. I can see my whole yard from here. Well, I *could* see it—if my fur weren't in my eyes. *Stupid fur.* Always getting in my way.

Scratch. Scratch. Scratch. My paws scratch the fur away from my eyes. *Scratch, scratch, scr . . . Crash!*

Wiggle, waggle, yikes! My stupid paws just knocked the ticktock toy, which was on the table next to the couch, onto the floor. I hop down to take a look.

The ticktock toy has a big crack in it. And it isn't ticking or tocking anymore.

"Look what you did!" I bark angrily at my paws.

Of course, my paws don't look. Or answer. They *can't.* Paws don't have eyes. Or mouths. Paws just have fur. Like the fur that got in my eyes and caused this whole mess in the first place.

Bump. Bump.
Bump. Bump.

That's the sound of Josh's two legs running down the stairs. Actually, he's *stomping* down the stairs. Which means I'm in trouble.

"Bad dog!" Josh yells.

See what I mean? I don't understand a whole lot of two-leg words, but I know what *bad dog* means.

I wriggle under the table and give Josh my best sad-dog face. "I'm sorry," I whimper.

Josh doesn't answer. That's probably because he doesn't speak dog.

My tail slips between my legs. It knows Josh is angry, too. Which is pretty amazing, since my tail doesn't have ears to hear Josh yelling. Or eyes to see his angry face.

"Sparky . . . ," Josh says to me, shaking his head.

His mouth keeps on moving. And I can hear sounds coming out of his mouth. But I can only understand my name, *Sparky*.

I know he isn't *too* angry, because now he's smiling. That's something dogs *and* two-legs do to be friendly. I guess it's okay to crawl out from under the table now.

Josh kneels down to scratch me

between the ears. I love when Josh scratches me. I think he must be the best two-leg scratcher in the whole world.

"A little to the left," I bark as I cock my head to the side. My tail pops out from between my legs and starts wagging wildly.

Crash!

Wiggle, waggle, yikes! There goes the tall, skinny glass water bowl Josh keeps on the table. I don't get how you're supposed to drink from that water bowl. You can't really get the water out, even if you stick your tongue all the way in. I know. I've tried.

Josh must think it's a weird water bowl, too, because he never drinks from it. He just uses it to hold flowers. Well, he used to. Now it's in pieces. The flowers are all over the floor. Water is everywhere.

"Sparky!" Josh shouts.

I turn around and bark at my rear end. "Stupid tail. Why did you hit the water bowl?"

I reach my head around and try to grab my tail with my teeth. My tail tucks itself between my legs again.

I reach back farther. My tail tucks itself tighter.

I reach. It tucks. I reach. It tucks. My tail and I are running around and around in circles.

"Grrrr," Josh grumbles. He grabs my collar and leads me to the backyard.

When he growls like that, Josh *almost* sounds like he's talking dog. I can tell he's saying I have to stay outside while he cleans up my mess. I'm pretty smart for a little puppy.

After he cleans up, Josh will probably get in his big machine with the four round paws. Then he'll drive away for the whole day.

But that's okay. Because now my tail and I can play, play, play! And there's nothing I like better to do than play!

CHAPTER 2

I race out into the yard. I have big plans today. I am going to dig the biggest hole any dog has ever dug.

Diggety, dig, dig!

The mud under my paws is cold and wet. Dirt flies everywhere. "Hey, Sparky!" I hear Frankie, the German shepherd who lives next door, bark at me through the fence. "You better cut that out. Your two-leg isn't going to like a big hole in his lawn."

"Josh won't care," I answer. "He only gets mad when I make a mess *inside* the house."

"That's what you think," Frankie warns. "I'm telling you, one too many holes in the lawn and you're going to the pound, kid. I've seen it happen a million times."

"I'm going to the *what*?" I ask him.

"The pound," Frankie answers with a laugh that sounds more like an angry growl. "You know, the place where they keep the dogs nobody wants. You don't want to go there—trust me. The dogs stay in big cages

with bars on the walls. And they don't let them run or dig."

"N-never?" I ask nervously.

"Not ever," Frankie answers.

Thumpety, thump, thump. My heart's beating really, really hard now. And my tail is hiding between my legs again.

Uh-oh. I have that feeling. That tingling feeling. And that means one thing—I gotta go!

I race over to the big tree near the fence and lift my leg. Sometimes I pee when I get scared. I'm *really* scared now.

"Don't frighten the pup, Frankie," Samson, the old mixed-breed who lives behind Josh and me, growls suddenly.

Frankie starts to say something else, but he shuts his snout right away. When Samson talks, all the dogs listen. Even a German shepherd as mean as Frankie.

Samson smiles at me through the

fence. "You're not going anywhere," he promises. "Your two-leg loves you. I can tell."

I believe Samson. He's been around a long time, and he knows all about two-legs. So if he says Josh loves me, it's true.

"Meow!"

I look up and spot Queenie, a neighborhood cat, sitting on the top of the fence.

"Hiss!" Queenie gives me a smug cat smile. Then she starts licking herself.

Cats are lucky. They don't have to take baths. They can clean themselves. Still, she doesn't have to be such a show-off about it.

I'll show her something *dogs* can do that cats would never try. I race over to a bright yellow ball in the middle of my lawn. I grab the ball with my teeth and spit it clear across the yard. Then I chase the ball all the way to the fence.

Woo-hoo! I'm playing fetch with myself. My tail perks up and wags really, really hard.

Queenie licks her paw and yawns.

I scoop that ball up in my mouth
and spit it out even farther this time.
Oooh yeah! I'm the king of fetch!

"I'll get you!" I bark to the ball.
My paws start running. Fast. Faster.
Fastest. I'm heading right for the ball.

Queenie jumps off the fence and lands in my yard. She takes one look at me and starts to run. *Yes!* Forget about fetch; Queenie wants to play tag.

"I'm it!" I tell her.

Queenie is a fast runner. But I'm fast, too. I chase her through the daffodils and across the pansies. I almost catch her at the rosebushes, but she turns around and heads toward my house.

"I'm gonna tag you!" I bark excitedly.

"Meow!" Queenie says.

"Here I come!" I bark back. "I'm right behind . . ."

But Queenie scampers up a tree. I look up to try to find her.

My fur falls in my eyes.
Bonk!

"That hurt!" I whimper.

"Meow!"

I roll over. There's Queenie, high in the tree, laughing at me.

It's not nice to laugh when someone's hurt. I don't want to play with Queenie anymore. I'd much rather dig.

Diggety, dig, dig.

Mmm. What's that smell? Beef? Chicken? Sausage? No, it's a bone! A bone that smells like all my favorite meats rolled into one. I stick my snout into the hole to get a closer sniff.

All I want is to take a bite of this supersmelly, meaty bone.

Chomp!

Wiggle, waggle, whew. Suddenly

I feel dizzy—like my insides are spinning all around—but my outsides are standing still. Stars are twinkling in front of my eyes, even though it's daytime! And all around me I smell food—fried chicken, salmon, roast beef. But there isn't any food in sight.

Kaboom!

W-what was that?

Kaboom!

If I were inside, I'd run and hide under Josh's bed. But there's no bed in the yard. And no Josh to keep me safe.

This is *wiggle, waggle, weird*!

Kaboom!

And scary!

CHAPTER 3

The *kaboom*ing stops. Just like that, the loud, scary sound is gone.

Slowly, I look around. *Uh-oh.* The big tree near the fence is gone, too. Wait a minute—the whole *fence* is gone! And where is my house? It's all gone!

My heart starts to *thumpety, thump, thump.* My tail hides itself between my legs. I put my new bone down on the ground and open my mouth and yelp, "Where am I?"

The two-legs on the street look

down and quickly move away from me. I don't blame them. I can bark pretty loud when I'm scared.

I raise my leg and a puddle of pee forms under me.

"How dare you!"

Who said that? It didn't sound like Frankie or Samson.

I spin around. Behind me is a small corgi walking with her two-leg. The corgi's eyes are opened wide, and her tail is down.

"Such behavior is inexcusable in front of the queen's house," the corgi says, wrinkling up her lip.

"I had to go," I tell her. "And when you gotta go, you gotta go."

"That is absolutely disrespectful," the corgi says. "Every dog in London knows not to do that."

Not *every* dog. *I* didn't know. In fact, I didn't even know that I was *in* London. Not that I know where London is, or how I got here.

I look over at the queen's house. It's ginormous! The house is made of stone and sits behind a black metal gate decorated with shiny gold trim.

I bet there are a whole lot of stairs to run up and down inside that house. And there are probably lots of comfy couches to nap on, too. A dog can get really tired running on the stairs. I can't wait to find out.

I run for the house. Fast. Faster. *Fastest!*

Bam!

Ouch!

"Stupid paws," I bark angrily. "You were supposed to stop!"

There's a tall two-leg standing just outside a skinny house next to the gate. He has a big lump of black fur on top of his head. "Hello!" I bark up to him. "Can you let me inside the big house?"

The two-leg doesn't move.

I stand up on my hind legs and spin around. But the two-leg in the red coat and the black fur just stares straight ahead. He doesn't even notice when I roll over. Or when I play dead.

The corgi drags her two-leg toward me. "Forget it," the corgi tells me. "He's not allowed to smile at you. He can't smile at anyone. He's guarding the queen."

"Why?" I ask her.

"In case someone wants to hurt her, I suppose," the corgi explains.

"That's weird," I say. "Whenever I'm around Queenie back home, *I'm* the one getting hurt. This morning when I was chasing her, I bashed my head into a tree."

The corgi gives me a strange look. "You chased the queen?"

"Yes," I tell her. "But she climbed up a tree, so I couldn't catch her. It wasn't fair. I'm not as good a climber as she is."

"The queen? In a tree?" the corgi says, shaking her head. "You're a very strange dog. All I can tell you is you're not getting past that guard. Buckingham Palace is reserved for the queen's dogs. *I* can't even play there, and two of the queen's corgis are my second cousins."

The corgi is such a show-off. So what if her cousins know the queen? If this queen is anything like the Queenie I know, she's nothing special.

"Oh yeah?" I bark back. "Well, I . . ."

I stop barking, and lift my nose high into the air.

Sniff. Sniff. Sn . . . Sausage!

My tail doesn't have a nose, but it must know sausage is near. It's wagging like crazy. A big, hungry drip of drool flops off my tongue. Oh yeah! I've got to get me some of that!

I scoop up my bone with my

mouth. But I'm careful not to take a bite. I don't want to see any stars or hear those big booms again. Not now. Not when I'm *so* close to sinking my teeth into some yummy meat.

Look out, sausage—here I come!

CHAPTER 4

I'm almost there. I can smell it.

Sniff. Sniff. Sniff. I smell something else. I put my nose to the ground.

Fries! *Wiggle, waggle, wow!* I put down my bone and gobble them up.

Sniff. Sniff. Sniff. There's that sausage smell again. I'm in food heaven!

I race off, but then my paws stop short. *Keep going,* I urge them. I look around and spot my bone. That's why they stopped. Smart paws. I have to find a safe place for my bone. Somewhere I can find it when I'm finished eating. I look right. Nothing. I look left. Nothing. I look down. Nothing. Then I look up and see a sign with a duck painted on it. And next to the duck sign is a big oak tree. Perfect! I'll bury the bone by the tree.

Diggety, dig, dig. Dirt flies everywhere. When the hole is deep enough, I drop my bone down inside. My back paws cover it with dirt.

Sniff. Sniff. Sniff. I smell food again. Follow that smell!

Sniff. Sniff. Sn . . . Bonk!

"Waaahhhh!" I hear a strange sound. What now?

I look up and see that I have bumped into a table where a bunch of two-legs are eating. And now the little two-leg is making a terrible sound. "Waaaahhhh!" It's hurting my ears!

Whomp!

"Owww!" Now *I'm* crying.

"Waaahhh! Waaahhh!" The little two-leg screams louder.

I turn my head to block the noise —and *sniff!*—the most unbelievable, giant chunk of sausage is under the table next to me. I dive for the sausage and take a bite.

"Owww," I cry again. My tongue is tingling. My cheeks are burning. My eyes are watering. "Ow! Ow! Ow!" I jump up, surprised by how spicy the sausage is.

Wiggle, waggle, whoops! I bang into the table. Plates of food fall all around me. Fish! Fries! Sausages!

I can't eat them fast enough. "WAAAAAAAAHHHHH!" A plate covered in ketchup lands on the

little two-leg's head.
He is really screaming now. And
so are the big two-legs. They are all
screaming at me!

I sniff around. The food is gone.
And so am I!

CHAPTER 5

I don't like this London place anymore. I haven't met one nice dog, or one kind two-leg.

Wait a minute. There's a two-leg standing over there, near to a big machine with four round paws. It's like the one Josh has. The two-leg is holding a yummy-looking bone, like the bones Josh gives me sometimes. And he's smiling, just like Josh does when he's happy to see me.

My tail peeks out and wags a little. Slowly my paws pad over toward the smiling man with the bone in his hand.

The man's smile grows bigger. I smile back at him. The man holds out his arms. I run right for him and then . . .

The man grabs me, picks me up, and throws me into the back of his machine!

The door swings shut. We start driving away really, really fast.

The machine bumps up and down on the road. I'm getting thrown all around.

Bump. Bump. Bump.

Oooo. My stomach feels sick. With each bump I feel something ooey and gooey race up into my mouth.

Bump. Bump. Bump.

Bleeechhh.

Uh-oh. The sausage and fries aren't in my tummy anymore. They're all over the floor.

And they don't smell so yummy now. I'm trapped with that stinky stuff as we drive off.

Wiggle, waggle, I wanna go home! But I'm not going home. The two-leg takes me out of the machine and throws me into a room with bars. "Let me out of here!" I yelp as loud as I can.

But the two-leg just walks away.

My paws start to dig nervously at the ground. *Diggety, dig, dig . . .*

Ow. There's no dirt or grass. It's just a cold stone floor. It hurts my paws just to scratch it.

There's no comfy couch to cuddle on here. Or any pillows to wiggle around in. And worst of all, there's no Josh here to hug me and scratch between my ears.

Suddenly I hear Frankie's voice barking in my head. *The place where they keep the dogs nobody wants . . . An awful place. Big cages with bars*

on the wall. They don't let them play or run or dig.

Oh no. It can't be.

But it has to be. It's exactly how Frankie described it. I'm in the pound!

But why? I didn't do anything that bad. I just ate some food and buried a bone in a hole. Then I remember what else Frankie said: *Two-legs hate holes.*

"This is all your fault!" I bark at my paws. "You dug that hole—two holes!"

"Hey, look, boys—fresh meat!"

I turn around and come face-to-face with three of the fiercest-looking bulldogs I've ever seen.

"Hello?" I whimper. My tail immediately buries itself between my legs.

"I can't believe they threw another dog in here," one of the bulldogs grunts.

"Just someone else we have to share the grub with," another barks angrily.

"Yeah! Like we *share*," the third adds. All three of them laugh.

I try to move away from the bulldogs. But they follow me.

"You can't get away from the Bulldog Boys," the largest one warns me. "We run this joint. Don't we, Buster?"

"Sure do, Bruiser," Buster answers him.

"We don't like strangers," Buster

growls at me. "What do you think about the newest addition, Barnaby?"

Who are these dogs? And what do they want from me?

The fattest of the three bulldogs waddles over and sniffs my rear end. "I don't like the smell of him. He stinks like sidewalk pizza."

"Like *what*?" I ask him.

"Sidewalk pizza," a small voice answers.

I turn around and see a little gray-and-white dog sitting in the corner.

"Sidewalk pizza is what Londoners call throw-up," the dog explains, walking over to me.

"You eat something, feel sick, and then it comes back up and lands on the sidewalk."

"Watson, just hearing your voice makes me feel sick," Buster growls. "Go back to your corner."

The gray-and-white dog pads back to the far-off corner with his tail between his legs.

"That's better," Buster laughs.

I don't like the sound of Buster's laugh. It's cold and mean.

"So what did *you* do to get thrown in here?" Buster asks me.

"I don't know," I tell him. "I was just eating. And then all these two-legs went crazy. So I ran away. But someone grabbed me and brought me here."

"Two-legs *are* crazy," Buster agrees. "But it's the *four*-legs that drive me nuts."

"You mean dogs?" I ask him.

"No. I mean the mini two-legs," Buster says. "Two-legs that crawl on all fours."

"He means two-legs' puppies," the gray-and-white dog explains.

"Yeah," Buster agrees. "The mini two-leg at my old house kept crawling around next to me and pulling my tail. Finally I growled at her. I mean, who wouldn't? But the next thing I knew, I was here. She pulled my tail and *I* wound up in the pound. There's two-leg logic for you. Two-legs are the enemy."

"No, they're not," Watson insists.

"We just haven't found the right ones yet. I know there's a family of two-legs waiting for me."

"You're full of fairy tales," Buster tells Watson. "You're never going to find that family you're looking for."

Watson looks like he's going to cry.

"That's not true," I tell Watson, trying to make him feel better. "I have a two-leg. He feeds me and plays with me and even lets me sleep in his bed. He's not bad. He's great!"

"Oh yeah?" Buster grumbles. "If he's so *great,* why did he put you in here?"

"He didn't!" I say. "It was the bone."

The bulldogs and Watson all stare at me.

"You got a bone?" Buster demands. "Hand it over!"

I put down my head and don't say another word. I don't want anyone to know where I hid my bone. I want to keep it safe, so I can go back and get it.

That is, if I ever get out of the pound.

CHAPTER 6

The Bulldog Boys can't be right. I can't be stuck in this pound in London. I have a two-leg who loves me back home. I have to get back to him.

Bam! I throw myself against the metal bars, trying to break free. The bars are strong. But I'm not giving up. I take a running start and then *bam*! I bang myself against the bars again. *Bam!*

"That puppy's crazy," Barnaby grumbles. "Look at him bouncing around."

"He's definitely full of beans," Bruiser agrees.

"I'm not full of beans," I bark back. "I haven't had any beans since that time I ate Josh's hot dog and beans off the table. That didn't go so well. My rear end was tooting all night long. *Toot. Toot. Toot.*"

The bulldogs laugh at me. But I don't care. I have to get out of here. I throw myself up against the bars again. *Bam!*

"Stop banging on those bars," Bruiser snarls at me. "It's time for my afternoon nap."

"You don't want Bruiser to miss his nap." Barnaby growls and bares his teeth. "He gets really nasty."

I can't imagine how much nastier

Bruiser could get. And I don't want to find out.

"The only thing Bruiser doesn't get mad about waking up for is food," Buster tells me.

"The Bulldog Boys will do anything for food," Barnaby says. "So I wouldn't be expecting any kibble today, kid. It's all for us."

I'm not going to argue with Barnaby. He's so big. And his teeth look very sharp. So I go over and sit with Watson. He's not so big. And he doesn't seem so mean.

"H-h-hi . . . ," I stammer nervously. "I'm Sparky."

"Hi," Watson answers. He gives me a little smile. I can tell he's trying to make me feel better. "The Bulldog

Boys don't know what they're saying," Watson assures me. "You'll get out of this place okay. You're a puppy. Two-legs love to adopt puppies. I've seen it happen before. It's grown-up dogs like me that have it rough finding a new home."

"But I don't want a new home," I tell him. "I want my old home. With Josh."

"I don't know about that, kid," Watson tells me. "Once a two-leg drops a dog off at the pound, he usually doesn't want him back."

I shake my head so hard it feels as if my eyes are going to fall out. "Josh didn't bring me here. It was that bone."

Watson gives me a funny look. "That's what you said before, but it doesn't make any sense."

"Yes, the bone brought me to *London*," I explain. "But a two-leg brought me to this place."

"A bone brought you to London," Watson repeats.

I don't think he believes me.

"I was *diggety, dig, digging* in my yard when I found this shiny, smelly bone," I explain. "I took a bite and . . . *kaboom*! The next thing I knew, I was in London."

Watson scratches his head with

his back paw. "A magic bone," he says slowly. "I've heard of chicken bones and turkey bones and steak bones. But never a magic bone. Are you sure that's what happened?"

I nod.

Watson scratches his ear. "Well," he says slowly. "It seems to me that if that bone is what brought you here, it's probably the only thing that will take you back."

My tail thinks that makes sense, too. It starts wagging wildly. "Yes!" I yelp excitedly. "All I need to do is go get my bone and take a bite."

That makes

my tail droop. "But my bone is out there," I tell Watson. "And I'm stuck in here. I gotta get out of this place. Right now."

"I've seen dogs escape," Watson tells me. "I've even tried it once or twice. Only trouble is, they always find you. And then you wind up right back here."

"*I* won't—if I can get my bone and go home *before* they find me," I say.

"Where is your bone?" Watson asks.

"It's buried under the tree near the big sign with the duck on it," I tell him.

"Where's that?" Watson wonders.

"Well, it's . . . um . . ." *Uh-oh.* This is bad. "I'm not sure," I admit finally. "But I know it's near that big house where the queen cat lives."

"The queen *cat*?" Watson looks very confused.

"The corgi said that the queen lives in the house," I tell him.

"You mean the queen of *England*?" Watson laughs. "I think you're talking about Buckingham Palace. I know where that is."

"Then you can help me find my bone! I'm going home!"

Woo-hoo! My tail wags happily. I reach back and try to grab it. But my tail plays keep-away. Tricky tail. It has me spinning in circles.

The three bulldogs open their sleepy eyes and grumble.

"Shhh . . . ," Watson warns. Then he frowns. "I'd like to help you, kid. But the two-legs around here get mad when you run away. They punish you when you get back. They give you a flea bath!"

I'm confused. "They bathe you in *fleas*?" I ask Watson.

"No," Watson says. "They bathe you to *get rid of* fleas. Even if I help *you* get home, they'll still find me.

And *I'll* wind up right back here. In the bath."

Thinkety, think, think. My brain is getting an idea. "Not if you come home *with* me," I say to Watson excitedly.

"What are you talking about?" he asks me.

"We can both bite the bone," I say. "And we can both go home. To *Josh*."

Now it's Watson's turn to get excited. "That's a great idea!" he says.

Bruiser opens one eye and growls. "Sit down and shut up, you two."

I know I should listen to Bruiser. After all, he's the meanest dog I've ever seen. But I can't. I'm too excited to sit and be quiet. Because Watson and I are going to do something Bruiser, Buster, and Barnaby never will.

We're getting out of here. We're going home.

CHAPTER 7

Wait. Wait. Wait.

Watson and I have been waiting a really long time for our escape.

At last, I hear two-leg footsteps coming down the hall.

"Here comes the kibble," Barnaby says. The Bulldog Boys all leap to attention.

A two-leg with a big bowl in his hands comes up to the cage. He unlocks the gate, and the door swings open.

"Run for it!" Watson howls.

"Right behind you," I bark back.

And with that we race toward the door. Watson is small. He slips right between the two-leg's legs and runs down the hall. I try to run around the two-leg. My paws are moving as fast as they can. My heart is *thumpety, thump, thumping*.

Oh no! My fur is in my eyes. I can't see where I'm going . . .

Bam! I slam right into the two-leg. He shouts and falls right on his rear end! The bowl flies out of his hands. Kibble flies up in the air.

"It's raining kibble!" I hear Bruiser bark.

"Dinnertime!" Barnaby howls.

"Food!" Buster adds as he jumps on top of the two-leg, who is still on the floor.

The Bulldog Boys are crawling all over the two-leg, trying to get the food. They don't even see that Watson and I have made a run for it.

"Hurry up, Sparky!" Watson barks as he runs down a long hallway.

I hear another two-leg shouting. He's racing up behind me. I run faster. There's no way I'm going to let him catch me and put me back in that cage.

"Run!" Watson barks.

My paws are *zoom, zoom, zooming* down that hallway. Fast. Faster. *Fastest . . .*

CRASH! My paws forget to stop when we get to the door. But for once I'm glad. Because when I crash into the door, it swings open.

"Good job!" Watson cheers as he and I dash out into the streets of London.

"Wahoo!" I yelp excitedly. My tail starts to dance around and around. "We're free."

"For now," Watson warns. "But the dogcatcher is going to come looking for us. And that means we have to hurry."

We run off as fast as our four paws can take us.

Sniff. Sniff. Sniff. I smell food! Meat. Fish. Strawberries. Bread.

Grumble. Rumble. My tummy wants some. Now!

"Can we eat?" I bark to Watson.

Watson stops in his tracks. "Covent Garden does have some wonderful scraps. Sure. Let's have lunch."

Covent *Garden*? This doesn't look like the garden back at my house. There's no dirt to dig in—only stone sidewalks. And there isn't any grass. Or flower beds. All I see are buildings and small stands set up outside. But those stands smell delicious. They're filled with food!

Plop! A two-leg walks by and drops a big piece of cheese on the floor. *Wiggle, waggle, wow!* I like this garden! *Mmmm.* I love cheese.

Toot! Toot! Toot!

What's that noise? Is it coming from me?

I sniff under my tail. Nope. It doesn't smell like beans.

Toot! Toot! Toot!

Someone is definitely *toot*ing.

Toot! Toot! Toot!

I see a group of two-legs blowing into shiny metal toys. The *toot, toot, toot*ing is coming from them. I wonder if they are full of beans.

There's only one way to find out! *Sniff, sniff, sniff.* I run up to one of the two-legs and sniff his butt. Just a friendly dog hello. "Hi there!" I bark.

The two-leg jumps up in the air. "AAAAAHHHH!" he screams.

"AAAAAHHHH!" I bark back.

Never sniff a two-leg's butt.

I look around for Watson. He's sneaking around catching fries, cheese, and cookies as the two-legs drop them.

SNIFF...

Then I spot another two-leg standing away from the crowd. He's not blowing into anything. And he's not making any *toot, toot, toot*s. He's throwing balls up in the air and catching them. He's playing fetch all by himself! But he's not smiling at all.

Josh *always* smiles when he plays fetch with me. This two-leg needs a

dog to play with!

"I'll play fetch with you!" I bark as I run over to the two-leg with the ball toys. "Throw it to me! Throw it to me!" I bark and jump up and down at his feet.

But the two-leg doesn't throw any of his balls to me. He just keeps tossing the three balls in the air and catching them all by himself.

"Throw the ball! Throw the ball!" I yelp excitedly. I'm still jumping up and down. I can't help it. Fetch always gets me all excited.

The two-leg tosses the yellow ball in the air. I jump up and catch it in my mouth. Then I bark excitedly and spin around with the yellow ball between my teeth. *"Wiggle, waggle, wheee!* Look at me!"

A whole bunch of two-legs come over to look at me. I think maybe some of them speak dog.

At first, the two-leg with the balls seems angry. He growls at me with words I can't understand. But then he spots all the two-legs who have gathered around us. They're smiling and clapping their front paws.

Now the two-leg is very happy to have me around. He throws another ball toward me. I catch it in midair and I dance around on my back paws.

The two-legs clap even harder. Yay! The crowd likes my new two-leg friend. They all start smiling and dropping pieces of paper into his hat. That seems to make him very happy. I don't know why. You can't eat paper. But I'm glad I could help.

The two-leg tosses more balls up in the air and catches them. One, two, three, four, five balls! They're moving so fast! I leap up and catch a green one in my teeth. The two-legs in the crowd start cheering.

I smile up at the two-leg. He smiles back down at me. We make a great team. I could play with him all day!

"Dogcatcher!"

Suddenly, I hear Watson barking

at me from behind the crowd.

"Run, Sparky, run!" Watson yelps.

Uh-oh. No more fetch for me. "Thanks for the game!" I bark to the two-leg. "It was fun! But I gotta run!"

Fast. Faster. *Fastest!* My paws are moving at top speed.

Boom, boom. Boom, boom. I can hear the dogcatcher's two legs catching up to Watson and me. He's running fast!

"Quick, Sparky, in there!" Watson shouts at me. He points with his snout.

I look where Watson is pointing. It's a tall, skinny red house. There's a two-leg inside. He's holding something against his ear. And he's talking. Who is he talking to? He's the only one in there.

"Hurry, Sparky!" Watson runs in

the skinny house and hides at the two-leg's feet. I have to hide, too. I run inside and stick my head up behind his coat. Wow! It sure is dark under here. I can't see a thing. I hope the dogcatcher can't see me, either!

"Aaaahhh!" the two-leg shouts.

"I wasn't sniffing; I was hiding!" I bark.

But the two-leg doesn't understand. He pushes me out of the way and races right out of the little house.

Ow! I bump my head on the glass window.

The two-leg doesn't stop to say
he's sorry. He just runs out of there,
tripping over Watson as he goes.
He doesn't say he's sorry for that,
either. "Shhh," Watson whispers.
"Stay very still."

I don't talk. I don't move. And pretty soon, I see the dogcatcher.

He runs right by us. He turns the corner and is gone.

"We're safe," I tell Watson.

"For now," he warns. "But we might not be so lucky next time. We've got to hurry and find your bone!"

He doesn't have to tell me twice. I run out of the little house as fast as I can.

Watson speeds ahead of me. He has little paws, but they can really move.

I'm right behind him. And then . . .

Sniffety, sniff, sniff. My nose smells a cookie on the ground.

But I don't stop. Not this time. Nothing is worth going back to that pound. Not even a peanut-butter cookie! So my paws keep on running.

No dogcatcher can catch me! *Zoom, zoom, zoomee!*

CHAPTER 8

"That was close," I gasp as Watson and I finally stop running long enough to catch our breath. I'm tired and thirsty. So is Watson. I can tell by the way his long pink tongue is hanging out of the side of his mouth with little drops of spit all over it.

Ding-dong, ding-dong!

What was that sound? I try to bury my ears in my paws.

"Don't worry," Watson tells me. "That's just Big Ben."

I look around for a big dog named

Ben. But I don't see anyone. It's just me and Watson, standing near a garden of flowers.

"Who's Big Ben?"

"I don't know," Watson admits. "I've never met him. But he makes that bonging noise all day long. You can hear him all over the city," Watson says as he lies down on the grass and sticks out his tongue. "It sure is hot out here."

"I know what you mean." I start rolling around on the cool grass. Out of the corner of my eye I see a two-leg watering flowers with a long green snake. It looks just like the snake Josh uses to water our flowers back home.

Wiggle, waggle, water! I bark excitedly. I run over for a sip. The two-leg turns to me and cups his hand at the snake's mouth so I can drink more easily. The water is cold and wet. *Slurpity, slurp, slurp.* I can't drink it fast enough.

"Sparky!" Watson barks nervously. "Get away from him. He could be from the pound."

But I know this two-leg isn't from the pound. He would have grabbed us by now if he were.

I guess Watson has figured that out, too, because he slowly walks over and takes a few quick sips from the long green snake. Then he backs away.

It makes me sad to see Watson so afraid. I can't imagine what it's like not to trust *any* two-legs. But I guess

it's because Watson's never had a two-leg to love him the way Josh loves me.

"Are we near the queen's house?" I ask Watson.

Watson looks around. "Not far," he says.

Wiggle, waggle, whoopee! My happy tail starts dancing again. Watson and I are almost home!

Watson sets off and I follow.

"There it is," I tell Watson. "It's the duck sign. And the tree!"

Diggety, dig, dig.

"It's right where I buried it." I bark excitedly as the magic bone appears in the dirt.

"That is some amazing bone," Watson admits. "I've never seen or smelled one like it."

"I know," I agree. "It's the best-smelling bone ever."

"And you just bite it, and the next thing you know you're somewhere else?" Watson asks me.

I nod my head. "We just have to make sure we both take a bite at the exact same time so we can go home together."

Home. The word makes me feel tingly all over. "You're going to love home," I tell my new friend. "There's always plenty of food and water. And Josh. Josh is the best part."

Just then, I hear footsteps coming up behind us. I grab my bone and dart into the bushes. It could be the dogcatcher!

I figure Watson must be right behind me. But he's not. He's where I left him, staring at two two-legs who are walking toward him. He doesn't seem scared. Maybe it's because it's easy to tell that these two-legs aren't dogcatchers. One of them is too little. The bigger two-leg looks like she could be his mommy.

I watch from the bushes as the little two-leg walks over and gently reaches out his hand to Watson. Watson looks up at him but doesn't move.

The mommy two-leg says something that I don't understand. But she doesn't sound mad or mean. She sounds nice.

Watson's tail must think she sounds nice, too, because it starts to wag. Watson walks over to the little two-leg and lets him pet his head. A minute later, the mommy two-leg scoops Watson up in her front paws.

Watson doesn't seem scared at all. In fact, he looks up and gives her a kiss with his tongue. The mommy says something to her little two-leg. A big smile breaks out on his face.

The next thing I know, the mommy two-leg begins to walk away with Watson in her arms. The little two-leg follows along next to them.

Watson lets out a whimper. It's very quiet, but I can hear him. "Home," he says happily. "I'm finally going to have a home."

Huh? "But you already have a home," I call to him. "With Josh and me."

"That's your family," Watson explains. "This one will be mine. Because they chose me."

I know how Watson feels. It's great to know a two-leg wants you. Like the way I know Josh picked me because I make him happy. It'll be just Josh and me again when I get back.

But right now, it's just me and my bone. Alone. In London. And the dogcatcher could be anywhere.

Ticktock . . . ticktock.

What's that sound?

I look down. Right there at my feet I spot a little ticktock toy. It has a crack in it, like the one I broke at home. But this one is still *ticktock*ing.

Josh would really like this! Quickly, I scoop up the ticktock toy and run back to my bone.

Thumpety, thump, thump, thump. Suddenly my heart starts to pound. What if Watson was wrong? What if the magic bone doesn't send me home? I'll be stuck here in London, all alone, without any friends—and with the dogcatcher still hunting me.

There's only one way to find out: I have to take a bite.

Chomp!

Wiggle, waggle, whew.

Suddenly I feel dizzy—like my insides are spinning all around—but my outsides are standing still. Stars are twinkling in front of my eyes, even though it's daytime! And all around me I smell food—fried chicken, salmon, roast beef. But there isn't any food in sight.

I wait for the big boom. The boom that makes me feel like I want to run and hide. The boom that makes me feel like I want Josh to hold me tight. The boom that just might take me home . . .

Kaboom, kaboom, kaboom!

The *kaboom*ing stops. Just like that. The loud, scary sound is gone.

Slowly I look around. There's my tree! My fence! And best of all, my *house*! It's not big or made of stone like the queen's home. But it's all mine. Mine and Josh's. Watson was right. The magic bone has brought me home again.

I wonder what Josh would do if he saw my magic bone. Would he take a bite? And if he did, where would he go? What if he didn't know how to get back to me? I don't want Josh to wind up in a pound. I better hide my bone so he can't find it.

Diggety, dig, dig. I dig a big hole right near Josh's new flower bed, drop the bone in, and cover it with dirt.

I grab the new ticktock toy in my mouth and run through my doggie door. Wow! There's my food bowl. And my couch. And my table. And my . . .

Josh!

Josh! Josh! Josh! I bark as he walks in the door. My tail goes crazy with excitement. *Josh! Josh! Josh!*

Boom! I'm jumping so hard, I

knock Josh right to the floor. But he's not mad. He's laughing and petting my head.

Then he notices the ticktock toy I'm holding in my mouth. He

reaches between my teeth and pulls it out. It's slimy with spit, but it's still *ticktock*ing. I stand there, looking at him proudly.

Josh stares at the ticktock toy. Then he stares at me. I wish I could tell him where I found the toy. I wish I could tell him about London, and Watson, and the Bulldog Boys. But Josh doesn't speak dog. And I don't speak two-leg.

So for now, all I can do is let Josh know how happy I am to be home. I don't need words for that. All I have to do is give Josh a couple of good licks to the face.

Slurpity. Slurp. Slurp.

Fun Facts about Sparky's Adventures in London:

Big Ben

Big Ben is the nickname for the bell in the clock tower at the Palace of Westminster. The clock has been telling time in London since 1859. There are four quarter bells in the tower that ring every fifteen minutes, but Big Ben chimes only once an hour. Big Ben weighs thirteen and a half tons, which is about the weight of a small elephant.

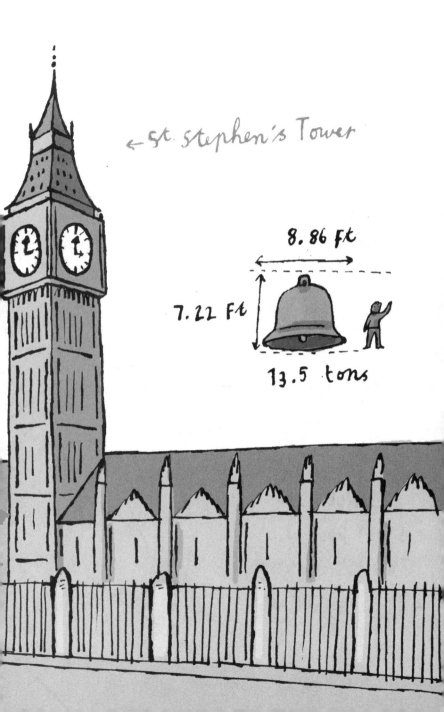

← St. Stephen's Tower

8.86 Ft

7.22 Ft

13.5 tons

Buckingham Palace

Buckingham Palace is the official home of Britain's Queen Elizabeth II. There are 775 rooms in the palace, including fifty-two royal and guest bedrooms and seventy-eight bathrooms. It also has its own post office, movie theater, doctor's office, and swimming pool!

775 ROOMS!
1,514 DooRS!
760 Windows!
40,000 Lightbulbs!

118 yards!

Covent Garden

In 1762, the Earl of Sandwich put a slab of meat between two pieces of bread and ate it in Covent Garden. Today you can get all kinds of sandwiches, sweets, and drinks in this area of London, which is known for its market stalls, restaurants, and street-performing musicians, jugglers, and puppeteers.

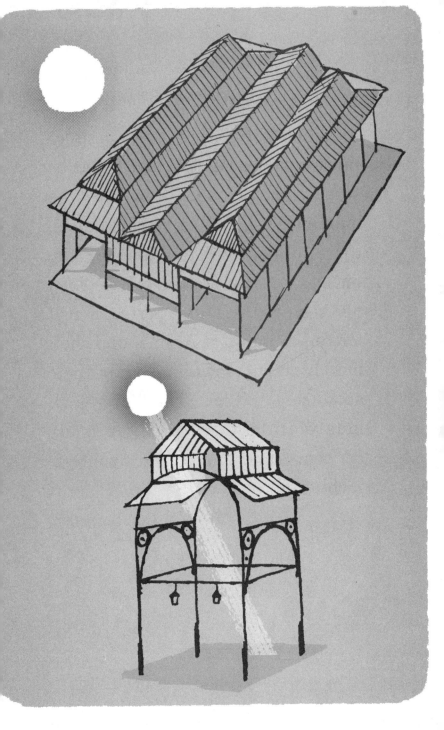

The Queen's Guard

When the queen is staying at Buckingham Palace, four guards stand outside the front of the building. When she is not home, there are two. Traditionally, the queen's guards do not move. They are required to stand perfectly still for ten minutes at a time, and then march up and down in front of their small sentry boxes. The furry black hats worn by the guards are made of bearskins and stand eighteen inches tall!

Don't miss another
Sparky adventure!

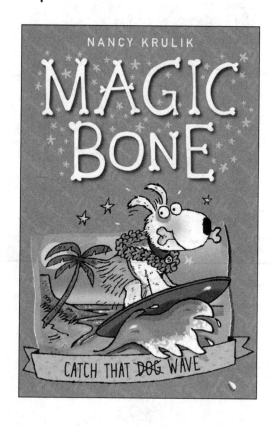

About the Author

Nancy Krulik is the author of more than 200 books for children and young adults, including three *New York Times* Best Sellers. She is best known for being the author and creator of several successful book series for children, including Katie Kazoo, Switcheroo; How I Survived Middle School; and George Brown, Class Clown. Nancy lives in Manhattan with her husband, composer Daniel Burwasser, and her crazy beagle mix, Josie, who manages to drag her along on many exciting adventures without ever leaving Central Park.

About the Illustrator

You could fill a whole attic with Seb's drawings! His collection includes some very early pieces made when he was four—there is even a series of drawings he did at the movies in the dark! When he isn't doodling, he likes to make toys and sculptures, as well as bows and arrows for his two boys, Oscar and Leo, and their numerous friends. Seb is French and lives in England. His website is www.sebastienbraun.com.